Baby For The Brundle Commander

Alien Baby Pact, Volume 3

Aurelia Skye and Juno Wells

Published by Amourisa Press, 2023.

JOIN JUNO WELLS' NEW RELEASE LIST!

Click on this link (or copy and paste it into your browser): http://eepurl.com/bnMJL5

Join Kit's Mailing List[1] (**www.kittunstall.com/newsletter**) **to receive notification of new releases and access bonus chapters for your favorite books. You get free books just for signing up. If you prefer to receive notifications for just one, or a few, of Kit's pen names, you'll have the option to select which lists to subscribe to at signup.**

---

1. http://kittunstall.com/newsletter/

Blurb

Brighton hoped for a permanent match, but her alien barely notices she's alive.

BRIGHTON HAS BEEN IMPATIENTLY waiting to be matched after her friends found happy endings with their alien mates. She's assigned as the proxy for brundle commander Dantel Oleig, but despite her high hopes, he barely notices her existence. She doesn't understand why he claimed her if he doesn't want a child or the possibility of a mate. The enigmatic warrior is frustrating, and it takes a catastrophe to get Dantel to open to her. Can understanding what drives him lead to a second chance, or is he too consumed with his mission for Brighton to ever reach him?

Seven years ago, the Faction agreed to save Earth from the Vorathan invasion in exchange for Earth women giving them one year of proxy rights to act as a surrogate, since the aliens of the Faction faced a dwindling population. With the Vorathans feared throughout the galaxy as bloodthirsty, vicious marauders, the Earth's government agreed.

That doesn't mean the women did.

Sometimes, you want to read about the entire alien empire and all its myriad twists and turns, immersing yourself in hundreds of pages of intrigue. And sometimes, you want to skip the frills and get to the main event. Juno and Aurelia are pleased to bring you a series of short, steamy romances about untouched human women making babies with their truly alien mates.

Prologue

WHEN BRIGHTON RECEIVED word Sarah wasn't returning to Earth either, having chosen to stay with her Palantir mate, she was happy for her friend, but she was lonely. She had been living alone in the POD for a few months by that point, and though it was nice to have room to spread out, since the pod was only intended for two and had been shared by the three of them for years, she missed having companionship.

That was what had led Brighton to reach out to her new roommate when she saw her scavenging through trash piles. There was something unusual about the young woman compared to the people Brighton knew, which made her wary but didn't send her running. Her pantsuit, though torn and dirty, seemed to be far more expensive than any garment Brighton had seen since the vorathans invaded. She'd approached the girl warily, asking, "Do you need help?"

Pei Ling, though she hadn't known her name at the time, had frozen for a moment and looked like she might dart away. Apparently, she'd found Brighton's small, curvy frame not terribly intimidating. Added with her wild mane of red-gold hair, she was hardly the picture of brute strength. She had hesitated and then approached, saying, "I'm hungry."

"Come with me." It was almost a surprise when the woman came along with her. As they'd walked, Brighton introduced herself, and Pei Ling had told her who she was as well. That was about all Pei Ling had told her then and now, though she'd been living with her in the POD for three months. She knew as little about Pei Ling today as she had when she invited the girl to stay with her.

Not to say they didn't have long talks, and she definitely considered them friends, but she didn't know anything personal about Pei Ling. It was a mystery she had hoped to solve, but her time was up. As Pei Ling prepared food from the synthicator, Brighton said, "I've been summoned."

Pei Ling froze for a moment, her fingers trembling as she turned away from the synthicator. "I'm so sorry, Brighton."

She gave a cheery smile. "I'm not. Honestly, I've been expecting it and looking forward to it. I know how happy Sarah and Violet are, and I'm hoping to find the same with my mate."

Pei Ling looked skeptical. "You're his proxy, not his mate. You can't always expect to end up with a happy ending, Brighton. All you have to do is be a sex slave for a year. Don't get attached."

"I'm just approaching it with an open mind." Brighton didn't care for the way Pei Ling was trying to dampen her enthusiasm, but she had observed during their brief acquaintance that Pei Ling was naturally more on the skeptical and pessimistic side. Brighton was sunnier and prone to see the positive in situations whenever possible. They still maintained a friendship in spite of their differences, and she didn't continue to argue the point.

"The POD will be yours now, so I hope you're all set." She was a little worried about Pei Ling living alone. The girl seemed to have virtually no survival skills, and Brighton had tried more than once to get an indication of her past. Pei Ling never shared it, and she'd stopped trying, but it hadn't diminished her curiosity.

"You'll be back in a year," said Pei Ling. She looked at the synthicator. "It has enough nutrients stocked for six months, right?"

"Probably. It was just refilled on the last government rotation." That happened twice a year, though sometimes, the schedule was a little off. More than once, particularly in the beginning after the Faction had arrived on Earth and started forcing the vorathans away from their planet, shipments had been unreliable. There had been times when she and her friends had gone hungry, but that hadn't happened for the last two or three years. "I'm not sure they'll refill it though. You're not officially listed as living in the POD, and if they think all three of us are gone—myself, Violet, and Sarah, I mean—they might not return."

Pei Ling looked scared for a moment, but then she stiffened her spine. "I'll be fine. I'm worried about you though. You're such a helpless romantic." She made it sound almost like an accusation.

Brighton laughed, unable to deny it. "I guess I am in a lot of ways. I'm just convinced I'm going to be as happy with my mate as my friends have been."

Pei Ling shrugged. "Good luck with that. I'll be fine without you." She sounded confident, though she looked a little uncertain. After a moment, she finished synthesizing their meals. She brought them over a moment later, and they ate mostly in silence.

Brighton was focused on the excitement of presenting herself at the embassy tomorrow to meet her match, and Pei Ling's thoughts were wherever they tended to flee when she was quiet. She didn't seem inclined to share, and Brighton had learned not to bother to ask.

Chapter One

BRIGHTON PRESENTED herself at the Faction embassy a few minutes early for her appointment the next day. She had brought a bag with her just in case she was taken right away as Sarah had been. Violet had a couple of days in between meeting and leaving, but she'd learned from their experiences not to count on any timeline. A proctor in a long black coat greeted her, and he seemed distant and completely unengaged in what was happening around him. "Brighton Fielding?"

She nodded. "That's me."

He marked something on the tablet in his hand and said, "Follow me."

She did without questioning to start with, but as they walked down a series of hallways and approached the Medbay, she said, "Aren't we supposed to stop for tea?"

The proctor paused to look at her. "Tea?"

"Both my friends who've been through this before had tea with their respective partners."

"Oh, the meeting ceremony. I'm sorry, but Commander Oleig has chosen to set aside the usual formalities. He's already signed the contract, and I'll get your signature in a few minutes. He's on a tight schedule and will be by to acquire you after your modification."

Brighton was stunned. "That's it? I don't even get to meet him first?"

If the proctor had any sympathy, he was good at hiding it. "Not this time. The Faction has the balance of power, Miss Fielding. You should accept that and do as you're told. Your year will be a lot easier for you. Particularly being paired with a brundle, you'll want to be disciplined."

Her stomach jittered slightly. She hadn't even had that much information from the email that had summoned her to the embassy. "He's a brundle then?" Her mouth went dry. "I don't remember much about brundles right now." Probably because she was so nervous, and her education had been fractured throughout the years, constantly displaced first by battles and then by resettlement and trying to reorganize into a cohesive society again.

"They're a warrior class, complete with the whole honor code and all that." He sounded bored. "They're big on following orders, so I assume he'll expect you to behave and do what he says. I've heard they can be stern disciplinarians, so it's better for you to just go along."

Sarah swallowed the lump in her throat. "Isn't there someone else?"

With a deep sigh, pausing outside Medbay, he pulled up her chart on his tablet. "I'm sorry, but your genetics most closely favor brundles, so you'll be easier to modify for surrogacy if you're paired with that species. The fewer modifications required, the more easily it is to undo them via epigenetics when your term of service ends."

"Great." She tried to stifle a hysterical laugh that came out more like a choking sound, which earned a look of concern from the proctor. She waved a hand and followed him inside a moment later.

While they waited for one of the medical team to acknowledge them, he thrust the tablet at her. "Sign."

She thought about refusing, but what was the point? If she didn't sign her agreement to the proxy situation, she'd find herself in jail until she was twenty-five, or a minimum sentence of seven years. One year with the unknown brundle had to be better than that. With a small sigh, she signed her name just as a mosaic alien gestured her forward, directing her toward an alphan waiting for her.

She knew from Violet and Sarah not to be too nervous about the genetic modification. It was a simple scan, which she had already undergone when she had registered, and the protocol would already be prepared. There was a slight sting from the shot in her arm as the alphan doctor told her in a smooth voice, "You'll hardly notice a thing. You might have transient aches and pains for the first few hours, but that's unlikely. It's an almost instant change."

She managed a small smile and said, "Thank you." She slid down from the table where they'd placed her. The proctor was already gesturing for her to follow, and he seemed impatient. She left Medbay with her arm sore and wondering just how quickly it would modify her hormones and reproductive system to be able to carry a brundle baby. She tried to tune deeply into herself but felt no change, and she exhaled in relief.

"You'll wait here," said the proctor after leading her into a sterile-looking room.

There was a metal bench built into the wall, and all the tile was stark white. "What is this place?"

"It's a docking room. Commander Oleig will be docking his ship and come to fetch you, so be ready." There was a slight softening of his features when he said, "Good luck." Then he was gone.

Brighton sat down, at first not minding the stiff and cool surface of the bench underneath her bottom. Soon enough, it started to feel uncomfortable, and she began pacing around to relieve the ache in her bum. She didn't think it was a reaction to the shot. Merely a response to sitting so long on a hard, flat surface.

There were no clocks in the room, but the wrist comm device she wore for communication when she wasn't in the POD marked two hours before the airlock door opened. She didn't see it, but she could hear it even from the room. There was a rumbling sound and a swish of air, and then the door closed again.

After that, there were footsteps in the hallway, and her stomach clenched with nerves and dread, though a hint of excitement, as she waited for her mate to present himself. She still had high hopes for this, and she didn't want to think of herself as just his proxy. She wanted a family of her own, and this brundle commander represented her best opportunity.

He entered the room without much fanfare. He looked at her for a moment and nodded his head. "Are you Brighton Fielding?"

She nodded slowly. "You must be Commander Oleig?"

He nodded. "I suppose should call me Dantel." He sounded reluctant to reveal his name.

She frowned in confusion as he stepped forward and lifted her bag. With his tall frame and bulging muscles, he made it look easy. She spent a moment admiring him as he turned slightly away from her. He had deep bronze skin with an undertone of orange, along with golden hair that fell to mid-back. It was currently confined in a braid, so it might be even longer once he loosened that. He wore a standard uniform, but his vest was sleeveless, revealing the bulging muscles in his arms as well. He could easily pick her up and carry her—or break her. It was a scary thought that she tried to dismiss. He didn't seem to have any interest in hurting her.

"Come along," he said briskly.

Feeling confusion and a little uncertainty, Brighton goaded herself to follow him, passing through the airlock. He didn't speak at all as they waited for it to close and the other side to open, and then they were in his ship.

She looked around, finding it rather utilitarian. She hadn't expected much else, since it was only a shuttle meant for one or two people. "What's the name of my temporary home?"

"My shuttle is called *Daytlien*. It means fierce in my language."

"It sounds pretty."

He sent her a look of disbelief. "I assure you, brundles do not value the sound of pretty things." His tone was dismissive as he walked down the hallway, leading her through the ship. A moment later, they arrived at what she presumed were his quarters, and her stomach twisted with a hint of fear and excitement. Would he expect to bed her right away? She was prepared, or at least she thought she was, but she wouldn't mind getting to know him first.

He opened the door for her and indicated she should pass through. When she did, he set her bag beside the door and said, "Put your hand on the biometric panel."

She did as he instructed, and he added access to the ship for her. Then he stepped back and said, "I'm sure you can find the galley and know how to use a synthicator."

Brighton nodded. "Would you like me to prepare dinner for us?"

"I have no time for dinner at the moment. Entertain yourself."

With those abrupt words, her alien was gone. She wanted to think of him as her mate, but it seemed like there was a great deal of distance between them, far more than the length of the shuttle. He seemed virtually uninterested in her, which was quite different from her friends' experiences. Their mates had been eager to know them, even if things had started awkwardly. Dantel seemed to have no interest in her at all, which hurt.

She occupied herself by finding the galley and preparing a meal, which she ate by herself. Then she briefly explored the ship. As she neared the bridge, a forcefield kept her from entering. She could see some of what he was doing, and he seemed to be programming a jump point route for them. She assumed it was to avoid vorathan detection, so he was using a roundabout way to find the Baxa homeworld. Perhaps it would add time to their journey—time they could maybe use to get acquainted.

When Brighton ran out of things to occupy herself, she returned to their quarters. His shower system was slightly different than what she was used to on the POD, but she was able to figure it out with the A.I. system's assistance. Once she was bathed and had brushed her hair, confining it to a braid to keep it from becoming a wild, tangled mess in bed—particularly during the throes of passion, which she'd read could be quite intense—she returned to the bedroom.

There was a frilly nightgown inside that she had bartered to acquire, wanting to make a good impression on her alien. She donned it and slipped into bed, trying to soothe her nerves. At first, fear of what was coming consumed her, but then irritation started to take over as it seemed less and less likely he was going to join her.

Another couple of hours ticked past, and she tried to occupy herself with reading, but her thoughts couldn't focus on the story. All she could think about was her mate had not come for her, and as it got later and later, she stopped trying to fight the urge to sleep. She bit back the need to cry, refusing to shed tears for the cold brundle commander with whom she'd been paired.

Pei Ling was right. She'd been setting herself up for disappointment by expecting the same happy ending as her friends had received, but it was all too obvious she was going to be little more than a burden to the brundle, and she couldn't imagine for the life of her why he'd chosen to accept her. He obviously had no interest in a mate or even a proxy to be surrogate for his child.

Chapter Two

DANTEL MADE SURE TO plot a complicated course to take them to Garris 12. He didn't want any of the stray vorathans to pick up their signature, and he certainly didn't want to alert Yaley he was coming. The last thing he wanted to do was give Yaley an opportunity to sneak away yet again as he had done every time Dantel had found him.

To ensure the route went smoothly, he slept on the bridge. He gave a passing thought for his proxy, but he assumed she would prefer to be left alone anyway. It must be awkward for her to be paired with someone she didn't know and expected to sleep with him right away. He had a modicum of sympathy for her, but mostly he left her to her own devices because he was so focused on reaching Yaley and finally punishing the vorathan who'd eluded him for so long.

By morning, he'd almost forgotten all about her until he heard sounds of movement in the galley. Realizing his stomach was rumbling, he yawned and stretched as he stood up, rubbing the sleep from his eyes. His body felt like he had slept in the same position for a few hours, which he had, but it was more pronounced now as he was getting older. A brundle his age should be considering with relish settling down on the home world and having a youngling, but Dantel wasn't able to focus on that goal until he'd finally dealt with Yaley.

When he entered the galley, she barely looked at him. He recalled her sweet voice and apparent concern yesterday. She had offered to synthicate for him, but she made no move to do so this morning. He grunted slightly, assuming her change in attitude was her dropping any pretense.

This must be the real her versus the sweet and slightly enthusiastic human he'd met yesterday, who'd seemed almost happy about embracing the idea of being his proxy. He hadn't believed it then, so it was far easier to believe how she presented herself now. Without another word to him, she slipped from the galley and returned to his quarters.

He ate quickly and followed her into the room. He was intrigued by the sight of her stuffing something that looked white and frilly into her bag, but she was dressed in more casual clothing, so he assumed it might be some of her personal undergarments. He tried not to imagine her in them, because he needed to focus on his mission.

He couldn't help sneaking a peek at her nicely rounded rear end as he passed through the room and into the bathroom to shower and prepare for the day. He was tired from his lack of sleep, and he blamed that and his inability to focus on his lapse as his thoughts wandered to his proxy. All he could think about was her having been in the stall before him, and the cleaning solution washing down her body. He wondered what her breasts looked like, and he wanted to feel them with his hands before grasping her hips and lifting her so he could take her against the shower wall. His cock was hard and aching with the thought, and it took all his discipline and a strong burst of cold solution at the end to bring his thoughts back in line.

This was why he hadn't wanted to claim his proxy yet. He didn't want to be distracted from the most important mission of his life, and he refused to allow her to interfere. After dressing in a fresh uniform, he nodded to her on the way out but said nothing. She didn't speak either, and he told himself that was for the best. They could learn to get along once he'd dealt with Yaley.

IT TOOK TWO DAYS TO reach Garris 12, and the night before they approached the planet, he entered his quarters. She was dressed in an unattractive sack-looking thing that he believed humans called a nightgown. It did nothing to display her beautiful curves, but a harsh reminder to himself to maintain discipline had him keeping his thoughts from straying to imagine what she looked like underneath it. "We'll be landing at Garris 12 tomorrow."

She frowned. "I'm sorry? I thought the homeworld was called Baxa."

"It is, and it's also several jump points from here. We'll be at Garris 12 tomorrow, and you'll be safer in the ship."

"Why did you bring me to Garris 12 instead of the homeworld?" She glared at him. "It's obvious you don't even want me around, so why am I here? Why didn't you just leave me back on Earth or let a different brundle claim me?"

"I have my orders. Grand Admiral Pate told me to claim my proxy while I had a chance. He's a wise man, so I followed him." It also been an implied exchange between them when the Admiral had agreed to have his people search for Yaley specifically when they were tracking all escaped vorathans. He expected Dantel to finish with his mission and then move on with his life. Dantel hoped it would be that easy, but he was far more skeptical about it than the Grand Admiral.

"You were ordered to claim me?" She tossed her hands in the air, clearly disgusted. "That's just terrific. I guess you weren't ordered to claim your proxy rights."

He frowned, wondering if she was miffed because he hadn't insisted on intimacy. "I apologize if you're offended, Brenda, but—"

She let out a harsh cry and scowled at him. "*Brighton*. My name is Brighton. You can't even get that right?" She shook her head and closed her eyes, seeming to be trying to calm herself. "This is just the worst thing ever."

"I shall do my best to ensure it's not too terrible for you, but my mission comes first." He refused to apologize for that. "I wanted you to be aware of Garris 12. It's not a safe place, and it's certainly not a nice place. When we're on the planet, stay in the ship."

She didn't answer or look at him. Instead, she reached for her tablet and seemed to be reading. He doubted she was absorbing much because she was clearly angry. The way her chest heaved, and her cheeks had flushed suddenly, made him realize just how attractive his proxy was. For a second, he was tempted to throw aside his blood vendetta and claim his proxy, take her back to the homeworld, and start the new life waiting for him.

Recalling holding his dying brother in his arms as they exchanged blood after he made the mark and promised he would find vengeance shut down that thought. As much as he was tempted by Brighton, he couldn't afford to allow his thoughts to veer away from the promise he'd made at his brother's death.

He would avenge his family's murder, and then he would perhaps have a chance to finally focus on the future.

Chapter Three

BRIGHTON WAS AWARE of the change in altitude and the pitch of the ship that clued her in to landing. She assumed they must have reached Garris 12, and he confirmed that a moment later by appearing in the doorway of the quarters she had been using. He had made no move to share them with her beyond using the facilities, and she told herself she was relieved for that after such a disappointing match.

"We've reached Garris 12. It's a true hellhole and one of the last refuges for the scum of the multiverse. Stay on the ship."

She nodded, not bothering to answer. She'd heard him the first few times he'd told her that, and she was still too angry to risk saying much. Unfortunately, Brighton tended to cry whenever she was sad or angry, and she didn't want him to think she was crying because he'd broken her heart. She was strictly enraged at the outcome. That was all.

With a heavy sigh, he closed the hydraulic door on the bedroom, and she heard the landing mechanism releasing the main door a few moments later. At first, Brighton intended to stay on the ship. It wasn't because she wanted to obey the brundle commander so much as she wanted to stay safe. After a couple of attempts to raise Sarah and Violet, both which both failed, she was at a loss of what to do with herself.

Communications on Baxa could still be spotty, and it could be weeks before she'd hear from her friends on a regular vidcall.

It was only through transmitted messages like emails or video emails that she often had any contact with them. She would have found it soothing to be able to explain the situation and get their advice. Not that either of her friends had any advice to proffer in this situation. After all, they'd both ended up in happy matches. At least their aliens had been interested in them from the start.

Deciding she was done wasting time sitting in her quarters, Brighton retrieved a few of the rathium scraps she had brought with her. They were pretty much a universal currency, but she left the few bars she had managed to save safely on the ship. She couldn't afford to lose her nest egg, especially since it was quite likely she would be starting all over again when her year of service ended. She doubted she had to worry about getting pregnant. That required an alien who actually wanted to mate with her, and the brundle seemed uninterested in anything but his mission, whatever it was.

For a moment, she worried she couldn't exit the ship, but apparently, when he had added her biometrics to the security profile, he had granted her access to everything. She was able to open the door, which extended down into a set of stairs that allowed her to step off the ship. Before departing the docking bay, she locked it again with her palm and then stopped to look around.

She didn't know what she'd expected, but it wasn't to be parked in the midst of several other shuttles. It looked like a mismatched conglomeration of new and old ships, and many had been hobbled together with replacement parts that clearly weren't a match with the original.

It was a little intimidating, and she avoided making eye contact as she walked away from the ship, since there were still people milling outside the other shuttles around her. As she walked away from the parking area, she heard sounds of merriment ahead of her, along with loud laughter, and she went that direction.

She was hoping to find a bar or a restaurant, but instead, she entered the fray of an open market. It wasn't quite like the open markets she was used to on Earth. There, people sold the necessities and a few luxuries, but everything was tightly controlled by Faction soldiers who patrolled to ensure there were no thefts. It was also clean and bright compared to this.

A strand of lights lined each side of the makeshift street, but the atmosphere was light on oxygen, and it was windy. Grit blew into her eyes, and she blinked and coughed as she tried to adjust. She hadn't considered she might need an E-suit.

Looking at her wrist comm told her she could technically survive the atmosphere, which she knew for herself, since she'd been outside the ship for a few minutes already. It was still reassuring to see the stats and know she wasn't too far from an ideal situation for survival. They must have terraformers somewhere on this planet.

She walked into the market, keeping her hand on the pouch of money attached to her pants. The risk of being pickpocketed at an Earth open market was high enough. This place seemed to have no discipline at all, so it seemed inevitable someone would try to steal her money bag.

At first, she browsed, though she did stop at one point to buy some type of alien fruit. The purple alien selling it to her had a universal communication device, so he was able to speak her language. "It's tasty," he insisted. "Completely safe for humans."

She passed a chip of rathium to him and took the fruit after he cut it open with a laser knife. It looked strange inside, and there were little squiggly things. She frowned in confusion. "Are the seeds supposed to move?"

The alien laughed. "How else would they pollinate? Pick it up and shake them out." He demonstrated in the air without fruit.

She picked up the rough-textured fruit, which had a yellow outside and a black inside along with the white seeds. When she turned it over and shook, the wiggling white seeds quickly scattered. Honestly, it was enough to temper her appetite, and she looked uncertainly at the fruit again.

"Eat. Delicious and nutritious." He smiled. "Totally safe for humans."

She took a bite, prepared to spit it out. It was a strange texture, but it reminded her vaguely of a peach. She smiled at him. "It tastes okay."

He nodded enthusiastically. "Completely safe for humans unless you have an allergy." He added that as an afterthought.

While she didn't know of any allergies, she quickly spat the fruit back into its skin. "Thanks." She moved on, tossing the fruit in a trash bin nearby. At least, she thought that's what it was. She was quickly disabused of that by a scolding shopkeeper, who picked up the fruit and hurled it at her. Whatever was in that bin must have been something sellable, at least to the alien, and Brighton quickly apologized and ran away, though she wasn't certain if the alien understood her.

She wandered a bit farther until she abruptly realized someone was following her. She noticed it when she stopped to admire a selection of scarves, and when she stopped again two tables over, the same group was still following her. They stopped when she stopped, and they seemed to think she was too stupid to realize they were following her.

She was conflicted about what to do. Of course, Brighton was terrified, but she didn't want to lead them back to the ship either. She wasn't even certain she could make it back there with them following her before they intercepted her. She looked around for Security, but there didn't seem to be anyone who was identifiable as someone to keep her safe.

Reluctantly, she realized she might have to communicate with Dantel. She paused near a large gathering of people, who were watching some kind of sporting competition between two aliens, hoping to find some safety in the crowd as she used her comm device. She didn't have Dantel's contact information, but fortunately, there didn't seem to be any other brundles on the planet. When she asked the computer to locate all brundles, only one showed up. He wasn't far from her, and she headed in the direction her comm directed.

When she arrived, she was at a seedy-looking bar. There were people outside behaving in a raucous fashion, and she was afraid to enter, but she was even more afraid to remain outside alone when the people who'd followed her were still behind her. They made very little effort to hide their presence, as though they were taunting her.

They obviously believed she couldn't handle them, and sadly, they were probably right. She didn't have the kind of training she needed. She had basic self-defense skills like any Earthling with common sense, but she didn't know how to take on three of them. They probably had weapons, and she was unarmed.

She slipped into the bar, her gaze darting around the various colors of aliens. Dantel's skin stood out amid some of the darker shades, and she made her way toward him. He'd tucked his hair up into a tight braid and clipped it to the back of his head, so she wasn't able to rely on the unusual shade of gold until she got closer, but she verified it was him as she sat down at his table.

He didn't look at her. He just said, "This table is taken."

"I know."

If it hadn't been such a serious situation, she might have laughed at the way he did a double take as he turned to look at her, looked away, and then back at her again with an expression of disbelief. "What are you doing here? I told you to stay on the ship."

"Clearly, I didn't listen. I got bored, and I wanted to see what Garris 12 was. There are three people following me."

He groaned, his gaze going to a back room. He cursed softly before he stood up. "Come on."

"What?"

"I'm taking you back to the ship."

She stood up, standing beside him. "That's probably the safest place to be."

he scowled down at her. "That's why I instructed you to remain—"

"I'm not yours to instruct, Dantel."

He glared at her. "Shush. I don't want people to hear my name. It might tip off Yaley."

She went silent, but she had a million questions suddenly. He took her hand, and it caused a shiver of awareness to shoot through her. She'd admired his physical exterior, but he'd been so distant and uninterested that she hadn't paid much attention to how she felt around him other than on a physical level. She still wasn't really analyzing emotions, but she couldn't deny a wave of desire swept through her when his hand tightened around hers.

He stumbled for a moment as though he also felt it. He looked surprised and glanced down at her before he yelled, "Duck." As he said that, he pulled her down onto the floor. A second later, something whooshed by. It was shiny and metallic, and she followed it with her gaze as it buried itself in the wall. It was some kind of knife or a similar pointed weapon. "Who did that?"

"Who knows with all the scum in this place? It could have been Yaley or your followers, or some random person." He sounded irritated as he kept his arm around her.

She looked around, spotting the three people who had followed her as they stepped into the bar. "That's them."

He sighed. "That's the direction from where the projectile came." He grabbed hold of her hand and looked at her. "Stay with me and behind me as much as possible. You understand?"

She nodded, clutching his hand. He pulled her to her feet a second later, and he started running. They zigged and zagged through the crowd, and as they neared the three people who'd been following her, he used his sidearm to blast one of them in the shoulder. The man fell back, and the other two suddenly looked warier. He held out his gun, easing her behind him as they backed out of the bar.

Brighton breathed a sigh of relief when they were outside, and the two remaining followers were inside, still watching. They looked unconcerned, which worried her. She tugged on his vest, but Dantel didn't acknowledge her. "Dantel, I thin—" She broke off suddenly at a sharp pain blossoming in her back. "Ow," was all she could manage to say as her grip slackened.

Dantel flipped around, scooping her up into his arms. He said something in his own language, and it sounded angry. She flinched, understanding she had inconvenienced him and risked his mission by not listening. She wanted to apologize, but it was suddenly difficult to breathe.

He started running. She saw him swing his arm behind him and heard the reverberation of his sidearm as he laid down cover. She thought she heard someone cry out in pain and hoped she hadn't imagined that. Whoever had stabbed her certainly deserved whatever came their way. There must have been four instead of three, and she hadn't seen the fourth one. Whatever their intentions toward her, they hadn't been good, so she felt no guilt for hoping Dantel had incapacitated them or worse.

They were back on his ship moments later, and he locked the door behind them. He took her straight to the galley, and she realized he also had a small Medstation there. "Strip," he said as he gathered supplies.

She did her best, managing to remove most of her shirt, but she was having difficulty breathing. "I can't get a good breath."

He stopped whatever he was doing and immediately strapped on the diagnostic gear. In seconds, the computer was reporting a projectile lodged in her back and puncturing one of her lungs. Blood was filling it rapidly. Fear consumed her. "I'm going to die."

"You aren't." his voice sounded kinder than it ever had. He seemed to be trying to soothe her. "We have an advanced repair system. You'll be mostly healed within an hour." As he spoke, he finished removing her shirt and undergarments, leaving her in her pants.

His gaze widened for just a moment as he took in her bare breasts, and she was certain he liked what he saw. He didn't let it distract him though. A moment later, he wrapped something around her. It was like a binding pad, and she drew in a deep breath as it made it even harder to breathe. "I can't..." She trailed off as the pain in her back lessened, though she was certain she started to bleed more heavily.

"It's removed the knife now, so the healing can begin. This part is a little painful, so I'm going to give you something to sedate you." As he spoke, he used a hypodermic to inject something into her arm.

She barely noticed it with the tight way the healing pad was clutching her, making it difficult to breathe for a different reason. She was scared, and she reached out without thought. When she took his hand, she half-expected him to shrug her off.

Instead, he held it, his dark brown eyes locking with hers. "You're going to be okay, Brighton."

She managed a small nod and held on to him until the sedative started to work. She didn't completely pass out at first, but it relaxed her enough that she was barely aware of what was happening around her, and her hand slackened around his. Before she completely lost awareness, she realized he was still holding on to her though he could have easily let go, and she probably wouldn't have noticed or remembered later.

WHEN SHE WOKE, SHE was in his bed. There was still a slight stinging sensation in her back, but she felt much better and only noticed it when she sat up.

"Don't move too quickly. You're still healing, and that could take a few more days. I don't have the full juice to run the healer at max capacity for long, but you should be able to manage until we get back to Baxa."

She carefully stretched, realizing the limits of her endurance and flexibility before the pain started. "I feel much better."

"You shouldn't have been out there at all." His anger must have returned now that his concern was assuaged.

She would have been far more concerned if he'd been angry the whole time, but he'd shown her a side earlier that maybe he hadn't planned to, but she'd seen and couldn't forget. "You can't just give me an order and expect me to follow it. I'm not one of your soldiers."

"If you were, you would know discipline. If you weren't injured, I turn you over my knee and spank your ass."

She laughed, startled by the claim. "You wouldn't dare. I'm an adult, and I highly doubt you discipline your soldiers that way."

"No, but I'm highly tempted to discipline my proxy in such a fashion. You put yourself at unnecessary risk."

"Yes, I understand I jeopardized your mission, and I'm sor—"

"You could have been killed." He roared the world words at her.

"Why do you care? You don't even want me here anyway. I'm surprised you didn't just leave me there to bleed out." As her tone matched his, she realized they were shouting each other. Fortunately, the *Daytlien* most likely had good soundproofing.

"I do care. You're my proxy. I want to take care of you, but I have to deal with Yaley first."

She shook her head, disappointed. "Whoever this Yaley is, he obviously means more to you than the opportunity to have a family of your own, so why don't you just return me to Earth or something? We haven't consummated anything, so I might be able to service another brundle, or maybe they'll let me out with time served." She couldn't help sounding bitter.

He flinched, sitting down slowly on the bed, though he kept his distance from her. "I'm after Yaley because of what he did to my mother, father, and two brothers. When the vorathans invaded our planet, they killed everyone they could find. I was one of the lucky few who survived, if you consider it luck. I was virtually alone, but I found my older brother. Vinden was on the edge of death, and I held him in my arms and made a blood pact that I would get vengeance. Once I have fulfilled the blood vendetta, then I can focus on my future. First, I have to deal with the past."

Brighton blinked, not having expected him to tell her anything, especially something so personal. "I see. I'm sorry." She genuinely was. "You should have waited to claim me until after you were done."

"Grand Admiral Pate had different ideas. He's accused me of becoming obsessed with my mission, and he agreed to help me expedite it but only if I tried to move on. Accepting the next proxy who was a match for me was part of our deal, and he wasn't about to let me forget that." His tone softened. "Please understand that I do want a proxy, and I look forward to the prospect of a child of my own. I also made a promise to my family, and in Brundle society, one doesn't break a blood pact. I have to deal with Yaley before I can move on."

"All right." It wasn't the pairing Brighton had imagined, and she doubted it would last beyond the year, but there was no point in trying to fight his inclination to fulfill his vow. Her family was also dead, so she certainly understood the need for vengeance. She hadn't promised her parents or her sister she would find the vorathans who'd killed them, but if she had the opportunity, she wouldn't hesitate to destroy the raiding crew that had killed her family after they invaded Earth. She didn't fully understand the significance of a blood vendetta or a blood pact, but it was obviously important to him. "How can I help?"

Dantel looked startled for a moment, but a small smile and a hint of grudging respect appeared in his expression. "As of this moment, I don't think you have any role in my revenge, save for keeping yourself safe on the ship. Will you agree to that?"

She nodded slowly. "Believe me, I have no intention of stepping foot outside the ship. It's too dangerous out there." She couldn't deny she was concerned for him. "Will you be safe? How many vorathans does Yaley have with him?"

"Intelligence suggests he's on the run alone, which makes sense. The Faction has been doing everything they can to chase down any remaining vorathans who haven't been pushed beyond the outer rim. The last thing we want them to do is gather a new foothold or regroup enough to renew their plundering and pillaging."

"I can tell you're well-endowed, um, engaged, er, ready to go up against of vorathan." Her face flamed with embarrassment at what she'd said.

His lips were twitching, but at least he didn't make fun of her slip. "I've been training for this since the Faction took me in. Once I have Yaley, I'll have no mercy."

She reached out and covered her hand with his. "That sounds like a good idea to me. If I had the chance to kill the raiding party who invaded my home and killed my family, I would." She closed her eyes, briefly remembering the terror of that day, which had come weeks after the vorathan had first started invading.

Her parents had tried to prepare, and they'd all hidden in the basement, but the vorathans had found them. She'd only managed to survive because her father had covered her with his body as he was dying, and the invaders hadn't bothered to scan for more life signs. She'd remained trapped under her father's body for a good hour, feeling his heat slowly dissipate before she'd driven herself half-mad with the knowledge she was covered in his blood and finally pushed him off her. It had been blind luck that the vorathans were gone by then.

"I would help you find them, but I suspect they're already dead if they were stationed on Earth."

She smiled, taking joy in that thought. "I know at least two of them were executed in public shootings. I was there to witness it." She didn't know the fate of the other vorathans, but she was reasonably certain they'd all seen justice. Any vorathan remaining on Earth was automatically executed when the Faction arrived to turn the tide. With the ferocity and the brutality of the species, no one made any attempts to try to rehabilitate them. It was impossible to do so.

"You should rest now."

She nodded, shyly patting the bed beside her. "You can share with me if you want. You look like you haven't slept well for days."

He heaved a sigh but nodded. "Yaley is unlikely to make a move in the daylight, so I might as well get some rest." He was just as cautious about lying down beside her as she had been to offer, and there was a vast chasm between them.

Rather than feeling safe, she felt bereft that he didn't lean over to touch her, but neither of their thoughts were conducive to sex or romance at the moment. Still, when she reached out a hand, she was only a little surprised when he took it in his own, gripping it tightly as they slowly fell asleep.

Chapter Four

SHE WOKE TO THE SOUND of screaming. Brighton had woken screaming from more than a few of her own nightmares, but she instantly realized it wasn't her voice. This was Dantel's. It was deeper, sharper, and full of soul-destroying agony. Without thought, she rolled over to bring her hand to his face. She cupped his cheek and gently started rubbing as she said, "Dantel, you're having a nightmare."

He stiffened, and his eyes snapped open. For a moment, he grabbed her wrist and held tightly, and she was afraid he might hurt her. Then awareness returned, and his touch gentled. "You shouldn't try to wake a sleeping brundle. We're trained to be ever-vigilante." His voice was hoarse, probably from the shouting.

She smiled, continuing to rub his cheek with her thumb. "I decided to take my chances. You sounded like you're being tortured."

He shook his head. "Same old nightmares... Memories, truly."

She nodded, and it was instinctive to lean against him. She snuggled closer, putting her head on his chest. "I have the same kind of memories too. I wish I didn't, believe me."

He put his hand on her head, gently smoothing his fingers through her hair. "I rarely have that kind anymore, but I suppose discussing the past stirred them up."

"I'm sure. I think I had a nightmare as well, recalling being trapped under my father's dead body as he used himself to shield me and save me, which is probably why I was so attuned to your nightmare. I think I was already waking before you started crying out."

He threaded his fingers through hers. "Sometimes, brundles develop such a bond with their mates, but this was probably coincidence."

"Undoubtedly." She wasn't hurt by his words because they were true. They weren't even close to mates yet. They hadn't even consummated their physical union. She bit her lip as she looked up at him. "Perhaps we both need a distraction."

He arched a brow. "What sort of distraction?" His not muzzle wrinkled slightly as he asked, clearly considering the options before them.

She grinned slightly as she moved her hand from his face down to his chest and started stroking. "If you can't go after Yaley yet, you have some free time, do you not?"

His smile grew, and he nodded. "I don't wish to rush you."

"I wouldn't mind a distraction myself."

"What about your back?"

She shifted slightly. "It's still a little tender, but as long as you aren't bending me over backward and doing strange things to me, we should be all right."

He looked intrigued by the thought, but he said, "I'll try to restrain myself."

With those words, she moved closer to him. The way his elongated face formed a muzzle, it was slightly interesting to figure out how to kiss him, but once they got into the groove, passion filled her. She'd never wanted someone so badly, albeit there hadn't been much opportunity in her life until now. Survival had taken precedent over romantic relationships.

Brighton was filled with a mix of fear and excitement as Dantel returned her shy kisses. The room was energized in a charged atmosphere that only increased with each second that passed. His breath was on her skin, and the heat emanating from his body made her heartbeat faster.

The kiss seemed to last for an eternity as their lips barely brushed each other, while their breath mingled, and a connection stronger than any force of nature formed between them. The world seemed to stand still, and only they existed, lost in each other's embrace.

Finally, they pulled apart, and Brighton's cheeks were hot with pleasure. She couldn't help but smile as she looked into his eyes. Warmth spread through her body, along with a sense of contentment she'd never felt before.

"You are sure you wish to be intimate? I don't want to rush you." He pressed a kiss to her forehead as he asked.

She nodded. "I'm sure. I want you...this, Dantel."

He smiled and his eyes were filled with passion. He pulled her close, and she felt safe and secure in his arms. With a gentle touch, he turned her to lie on her back, being careful of the wound that was still healing.

Dantel kissed her neck and trailed his lips down her body as his hands caressed her curves and heightened her senses, sending pleasure through every nerve ending in her body. The desire to be closer to him overwhelmed her. He pulled back long enough to undress, and she did the same, though she was only wearing pants and underwear thanks to needing to be nude from the waist up for the healing system.

He laid down again and returned his attention to her lips to kiss her again, slower this time. His hands moved around her back, pulling them even closer together than before, though he steered well clear of the wound.

His heart raced against her chest as their embrace intensified. He rolled onto his back, taking Brighton with him so that she straddled him while they stayed intertwined in each other's arms.

"You're beautiful, Brighton. I didn't dare dream of having my own mate or proxy while focusing on finding Yaley. Having you here with me is amazing."

"I feel blessed too." She bent her head to kiss him again. His lips parted, and her tongue surged inside to explore his depths. He let her explore until he seemed unable to remain so passive. He broke the kiss and trailed his tongue down her chin to nip her neck.

Dantel's hands moved down her body as the rest of him followed at a more sedate pace, caressing her curves and sending shivers through her. His touch was gentle, but firm, and each caress seemed to unlock something within her, allowing her to give in to the pleasure of his touch.

He moved lower and lower until his mouth was on her, and her breath caught in her throat as he began to explore her pussy. His tongue moved in slow circles, teasing and sending waves of pleasure through her. Her body quivered with anticipation as he increased the intensity of his licks and sucked on her sensitive nub.

His muzzle and tongue moved in perfect harmony, and her body tensed in pleasure as her orgasm built. His hands moved up to her hips, holding her firmly in place as he increased the intensity of his movements, pushing her closer and closer to the brink of ecstasy. Finally, the wave of pleasure crashed over her, and she screamed out in pleasure as her orgasm took over her body. She shuddered and convulsed as the sensations slowly subsided, leaving her in a blissful state of relaxation.

"Come here," Dantel said softly, beckoning her to him. She complied, and he gathered her in his arms, pulling her close to him. They embraced in a timeless bubble as the aftermath of passion slowly faded.

After a few moments of cuddling and caressing, Dantel shifted so that he was behind her on his hands and knees. He held her hips as he prepared to enter her from behind, and Brighton felt a new wave anticipation, even as the first thrust brought a surge of pain. "It hurts." She pressed her head into the pillow.

"I know. I've heard it can be painful the first time for many female species. It's my first time as well."

That startled her, though she supposed it shouldn't. The Faction had few females in their races. "Does it hurt you?"

"No. It's so amazing I can barely hold on."

She smiled at that, wiggling her hips, and discovering it no longer hurt to have him inside her. "Then don't hold back."

Dantel began to move, and Brighton gasped in pleasure with each thrust. His movements were slow and controlled at first, but as he increased the intensity and speed, she found herself rising to meet him.

He was soon wild and untamed but still gentle with her, and Brighton's emotions started to swell. She dared cling to the tentative hope that she might still end up as more than his proxy.

"I can't hold back." He grunted those words as his fingers dug almost painfully into her hips. He thrashed and thrust deeply inside her, driving her pleasure higher and higher. Eventually, the sensations of pleasure became too much for Brighton, and she screamed as another climax raced through her. Dantel tensed and then relaxed as his orgasm followed hers, with him spilling his seed inside her.

Afterward, they laid with their bodies still connected and their hearts beating in tandem amid the panting and sweating from the aftermath of their lovemaking. It was a beautiful moment, and Brighton felt closer to Dantel than ever before.

Brighton's eyelids were getting heavy, and she snuggled closer to Dantel. "That was incredible," she said, her voice still unsteady with emotion.

"It was." Dantel pulled her closer and placed a gentle kiss on her forehead. "It was perfect."

"Do you think we can make this work?" she asked hesitantly.

He looked at her intently, a flicker of hope in his eyes as he affirmed what she was asking him. "Yes," he said firmly, taking one of her hands in his and holding it close to his heart.

"Once I've dealt with Yaley, I promise I'll do everything I can to make this work between us." He leaned forward and kissed her again before snuggling back into her embrace once more. He pulled her closer to him and whispered against her forehead, "Sleep now. You need rest and protein to recover."

"From sex? I believe it."

He laughed. "From your stabbing, Brighton."

She flushed, glad he didn't see that from the position they were now in, since it was embarrassing to have forgotten all about the wound. "I'll be all right."

"You will be." He sounded confident.

Brighton's last thought before sleep overtook her was she seemed well on her way to having her own happy ending, just as Violet and Sarah had experienced.

BRIGHTON HAD BEEN SO certain they were on their way to bonding and creating a deep connection after their amazing lovemaking, so it was quite disappointing to wake alone. The only indication he'd been there, besides the new achiness in her body, was a protein shake on the bedside. He was gone, no doubt after Yaley, and while she understood his mission, she couldn't help being hurt that he hadn't at least woken her to say he was leaving. What if he was injured or killed? She'd have no way to know, and she couldn't even fly herself away from Garris 12. Likely, she'd be able to raise help from the Faction, but she would be trapped here until then.

Realizing she was using practical thoughts as a way to distract herself from dealing with the betrayal and sadness filling her, she pushed it all aside. She allowed herself a few minutes to grieve him not staying or leaving with no word of parting.

She reminded herself he was a warrior first and foremost, and his blood pact meant everything to him. He was unaccustomed to answering to someone else aside from his chain of command. Perhaps he would find a way to change over their time together, and she had a hint of hope after he had been so tender with her during lovemaking. She had to cling to what could be instead of hurting herself by analyzing what had happened.

She heard the ship opening a moment later, and she hurriedly stood and dressed. She wanted to tell him her thoughts, and to express her anger that he hadn't bothered to wake her before leaving. Mostly, she hoped to be able to celebrate his victory with him as he she left the quarters and walked toward the shuttle door. They couldn't truly begin until he'd ended Yaley.

Chapter Five

DANTEL WOKE BEFORE Brighton, and he couldn't bring himself to wake her. She looked so peaceful, and she was still healing. He knew rest and protein would facilitate that even faster, so he left a protein drink on the bedside table beside her before dressing and leaving the ship. It was dark enough now that Yaley would feel more confident moving around, so he made his way back to the bar.

As he got closer, he saw a bloodstain on the dirt, assuming it was from one of the would-be robbers who had attacked them earlier. He felt no remorse as he stepped over it as many other people were doing. It was already starting to disappear into the grime of the street, and by morning, no one would probably even know it was there. He thought that was a fitting end for the kind of lowlife scum who would stalk and attack an innocent woman.

When he entered the bar, he went straight to the bartender. He'd made contact the night before, giving the man a generous tip, and the serp in front of him nodded in acknowledgement. "He's in the back," he said with a slight hiss as his forked tongue flicked out. "I've been giving him extra strong drinks as you instructed."

"Thanks." He put down an entire rathium bar on the countertop, and the bartender did a neat trick by making it instantly disappear into his pocket.

"Would you like a drink?"

Dantel shook his head. "Nothing alcoholic anyway. I suppose I should blend in, but I want to keep a clear head."

The serp nodded and quickly poured him something that appeared to be tonic water. He took a sip, and it had an unpleasant metallic taste, indicating the water was drawn from the planet itself, but he wasn't going to be too picky since he had no intention of actually drinking it. He lifted the glass in a slight toasting motion to his bartender. "Thanks for your help."

"Try not to tear up the place too badly."

"I think you can cover the repairs if I do." He looked at the bartender's pocket, where the rathium bar now rested.

The serp nodded and turned to his next customer.

Dantel faded into the crowd, gradually working his way to the back room. If it was like most of these establishments, that was where the worst things happened—gambling, back room deals, and the very heart of the villainy planned in such places. He wasn't at all surprised to find it was Yaley's preferred hangout.

When he slipped into the back room, he almost expected to be challenged by someone guarding it, but they didn't have that kind of security. Apparently, they relied on the villains to regulate and secure themselves. That was to his advantage, because he doubted Yaley would find any allies among the thieves surrounding him.

He was further encouraged when he noticed Yaley was currently involved in a complicated wagering based on a Grimlock game. He was having a heated argument with those at the table, trying to insist he had won. Dantel's UCD quickly translated they were accusing Yaley of cheating.

It seemed like a good time to wade in, and he walked over and slammed down his drink on the table. "I guarantee you gentleman...and lady," He nodded to the alphan woman sitting at the table, "That this lowlife is certainly cheating. I expect you all have a claim to him, but I have an older claim." As he spoke, he opened his palm to reveal the scar there. It was carved in the vendetta symbol, and it matched the one he had left on his brother's hand as Vinden was dying. "I have a blood vendetta."

That caused most of the aliens around them to scatter. The alphan female cast a glance between them for a moment and asked, "Do you need assistance with him?"

He shook his head. "No. Yaley is all mine."

"I'll leave him to you then." With that, she was gone. Everyone else had picked up on the mood and scattered too, and it was just the two of them in the back room.

He didn't give Yaley a chance to do much. Dantel launched himself at the other man, grabbing hold of his shoulder and biting hard. He shook him with his muzzle, making Yaley scream. HIs tough vorathans scales were hard to bite through, but Dantel had good brundle teeth and a strong edge of determination. Seconds later, Yaley's blood squirted in his mouth, and it was a deeply satisfying sensation, though he turned his head and spat it out.

That was all the distraction Yaley needed. One second, he was pinned under Dantel, but the next, Dantel cried out and jerked back as his entire body began to convulse under the force of electronic voltage passing through the shocker Yaley had hidden.

As Yaley scrambled up and started running, Dantel did his best to focus on regaining control of his body under the constant force of the electronic spasms. After a second, he let out a harsh cry as his fingers dug into the prongs, and he managed to wrench off the weapon. The cessation of spasms was almost painful in its own right for a moment, but after he shook his head and regained his focus, he ran after Yaley.

No one tried to block him, but no one had tried to stop Yaley either. He was surrounded by a group of slightly interested bystanders, but none of them were going to interfere. He'd declined the only offer of help he'd had, but he was determined to take Yaley alone.

He followed Yaley, easily detecting his path from both scent and the blood drops the vorathan left behind. He was starting to grow alarmed as the trail led to his ship. When he reached the shuttle a moment later, he was horrified to see the door standing open. He had good security, but Yaley must have a device that bypassed his security protocol. He wasn't worried about his ship.

His first thought was for Brighton, and he raced up the stairs, shouting her name. He'd barely entered the ship when he skidded to a halt. The sight before him made him sweat as his stomach clenched with nausea. "Let go of her."

Yaley held Brighton against him, one of his thick claws pressed against her carotid artery. "I know why you're after me. I've gathered that much over the years. I must have killed your family." Yaley laughed, but it was a cold and heartless sound. "I've killed thousands of families. What makes yours so special?"

He lifted his palm and showed him the scar there. "I swore a blood vendetta to destroy you, and it's finally time."

"Not really. I have your mate in my arms. I can smell you all over her, but it won't take much to remove your scent and replace it with mine." As he said that, his obscenely long tongue flicked out and slurped over Brighton's cheek. She let out a cry of disgust, but in a second, she made Dantel prouder than he'd ever imagined. As the tongue was flitting away from her, she lunged forward and bit down hard.

Yaley squealed in surprise and pain, trying to push her back. She was clamped on pretty tightly, and by the time he succeeded in knocking her loose, Dantel was behind him. He didn't have to think about it. He just acted by punching through Yaley's back to remove his heart. It was still pulsing in his hand when he pulled it out through his back and spun Yaley to face him. Feeling a surge of dark glee, he opened Yaley's mouth and shoved his own heart inside, watching as the last of the life ebbed from Yaley's eyes while his heart stopped beating. When it was over, he picked up the carcass and tossed it out of his ship before closing the door.

When he turned to Brighton, he expected to find her horrified. Instead, she launched herself at him, peppering his face with kisses and holding tightly to him. She didn't seem concerned about the blood covering him, so he picked her up and carried her straight into the shower, where they cleaned themselves before he claimed her again.

When they'd finished, he carried her into the bedchamber and laid down beside her. "It's over."

She nodded, taking his hand and rubbing her thumb across the scar on the palm. "How do you feel?"

"Good. Savage in some ways." He flashed a grin that showed just a hint of his teeth. "Somewhat empty though. I spent so long chasing him, and then it was over so quickly..."

She laughed. "He probably didn't think it was all that fast in the last few seconds of his life."

Seeing the enjoyment she took from his enemy's death only made him want her even more. He pulled her closer and kissed her before lifting his head. "You are utter perfection, Brighton. I couldn't ask for a better mate if I had designed one."

She laughed as she cuddled closer. "I'm just your proxy, remember?"

He growled low in his throat. "You're my mate. I'm claiming you in the old ways." As he said that, he positioned her beneath him and entered her in one hard thrust. She was still wet from before, and she accommodated him easily.

She didn't try to pull away. Instead, she pulled him closer, digging her nails into his buttocks. "We don't know each other."

"We'll learn everything we need to know." He bent and suckled on her neck, making her moan with satisfaction. "Do you deny my claim?" He held his breath, hoping she wouldn't. He'd have to honor her refusal, but that didn't mean he'd give up trying to convince her.

"I don't." She sighed and leaned against him, relaxing her body as she started to thrust urgently. "This is what I wanted. I wanted a mating that would last for life and my own happy ending. Violet and Sarah are so happy with their mates that that's what I wanted and hoped for."

"I'm sorry I was so distant and uninterested in the beginning. Yaley had consumed my life, and now I see I had focused too much on my pact. I understand why Grand Admiral Pate wanted me to move on."

"Now you can, secure in the knowledge you've fulfilled your vow to your brother and killed Yaley. There's no reason we can't focus on the future and build a happy one together. We can be happy together, can't we, Dantel?" Her orgasm crested as she asked, and she squeezed around him.

He gripped her hips and thrust forcefully in and out of her until he was on the cusp of coming. When her fold squeezed around him, he let go with a roar. "Mine."

"I'll take that as a yes," she said with the laugh as she pulled him so close they were practically one being. He realized that was just what he wanted—to merge and become one with the human beneath him. He was certain their future would be happy.

When their frenzied mating was over, he stood up and said, "There's one more thing I have to do." He braced himself for her reaction as he said, "I need to claim his head."

She only looked mildly interested. "Why?"

"It's brundle custom to mount the head of our enemies on our wall, particularly when it's at the cessation of a blood pact."

She grimaced slightly. "That's going to make for some interesting interior decorating." She yawned and stretched.

He arched a brow. "That's all you have to say?"

She nodded, looking content. "It's your custom, and I respect that."

With a pleased laugh, he quickly threw on his pants and went outside to fetch the head. The body was where he'd tossed it, and it didn't take his laser knife long to sever the head from the rest of the carcass. He claimed it, wrapped it in a cloth, and stuck it in the hold. She might know about it, but she didn't need to deal with it until it had been treated and mounted.

Then he returned to his mate. What had once been a bleak existence stretching before him suddenly seemed full of promise, and he couldn't wait to get on with the next steps of his life with Brighton.

Epilogue

Six years later...

DANTEL HAD THEIR OLDEST son, Vinden, with him. He was teaching him how to track, wanting him to know some of the old ways of the brundle, though there wasn't much opportunity to hunt on Baxa. Mostly, they farmed and led a peaceful existence, and he appreciated that. They would have to return for an Earth rotation next year, and he would miss their homeworld while they were back on Earth, though Brighton was looking forward to introducing their three children to the Earth side of their heritage. For his part, he would have happily remained on Baxa, but his duty called, and he would answer.

"There it is," said Vinden. He was excited as he pointed to the hooved animal they'd been tracking. The species was officially designated Baxa-1187, but Brighton had assured him it looked a lot like an Earth deer.

"Very good."

"Should I shoot it?" Vinden sounded undecided about such a course and looked anxious. He had his mother's eyes, though that and her hair were about the only things he'd inherited from her. He definitely had his mother's softer heart though, and even if there had been a need to hunt on Baxa, Dantel might not have been able to entice his son to learn. He ruffled the boy's red-gold curls, which were the only other sign of human input in his heritage and said, "That won't be necessary."

Vinden breathed out a sigh of relief. "I didn't really want to shoot it, and I sure didn't want to put it on the wall."

He smiled as he put his arm around his son's shoulders and led him back to the POD they had extended to a full-sized dwelling for their growing family over the last six years. "We only mount the heads of our enemies on the wall."

"Like Yaley," said Vinden. He'd already asked when he was barely learning to speak why there was a head on the wall, and he had taken it in stride when Dantel explained it was a brundle tradition.

"Precisely."

When they entered the dwelling, his daughter was playing on the floor with a set of wooden blocks he'd carved from one of the trees on their homestead. She looked up at him and smiled. At four, she was a petite thing, far smaller than the usual brundle, but that was owing to getting some of her mother's genetics. She said, "Mommy's in Aril's room."

He bent down and scooped up his daughter, kissing Chantel on the cheek. "Let's go find her."

She nodded her agreement, clinging to him as the three of them walked through the house. They entered the baby's room a moment later, and he found his wife nursing. Aril was only a few weeks old, but he already seemed large in her arms. He was going to be more along the lines of a brundle build than a human build, and he had an appetite to match.

He looked down with pride for a moment, running his finger over Aril's plump cheek before lifting his hand to cup Brighton's cheek as he stroked his thumb across her chin. "How are you, my love?"

She smiled, looking tired but content. "I'm well. How did our son deal with tracking?" She winked at Vinden.

"I found the Baxa-1187," said Vinden proudly. "We didn't shoot it though, Mom."

Brighton smiled her approval. "I'm glad to hear that. I thought shooting it might be the brundle custom."

Dantel laughed. "Sometimes, the brundle are willing to try new ways." Thank goodness for that, or he wouldn't have his cherished mate, his children, or the new life they'd built on Baxa.

"Sarah and Violet have both confirmed they'll be here for Aril's welcoming ceremony." She seemed excited.

He nodded, please to hear that. Over the years, he'd become friends with Reld and Shaw, and he looked forward to seeing them again. His children would be anxious to play with theirs as well. "Will Pei Ling come too?"

"I haven't heard back from her yet, but I hope she will."

"It'll be nice to see our friends, but you know I'm content with just our small family." He ran a hand through her hair as he whispered that.

"So am I." She lifted her head, and he kissed her.

"Gross," said Vinden as Chantel giggled.

"Not at all. Someday, I hope you'll have a mate too, my son." He ruffled the boy's hair again as he offered Brighton a hand to assist her to stand. "Come. Vinden and I will synthicate dinner, and we'll play that horrible Earth game you like so much."

"*Monopoly*?"

He shuddered, just imagining the horror of his next few hours, but he nodded. "That's the one."

"I love you." She put her arm around his waist as they walked to the main part of the dwelling.

"I love you too, my mate." Ignoring his son's sounds of disgust, he pulled her into his arms and gave her a proper kiss. Then they spent the evening quietly, as a family, and he'd never been happier, even if it meant he had to play *Monopoly*.

About Juno

JUNO WELLS GREW UP on Florida's Space Coast, watching the shuttles take off from Cape Canaveral. When she hit college, her childhood fantasies about space travel turned highly romantic. Now her mind reels with space adventures of fantastic alien lords in distant galaxies, and the earth women they love.

Wells' stories explore the complex, sensual relationships between inhabitants of different star systems. There are always happy endings just as there is always a new world to explore.

Have a comment? Make first contact with Juno at authorjunowells@gmail.com.

About Aurelia

AURELIA SKYE IS THE pen name *USA Today* Bestselling author Kit Tunstall uses when writing science fiction romance, paranormal romance, and paranormal women's fiction. It's simply a way to separate the myriad types of stories she writes so readers know what to expect with each "author."

[Website](1)

---

1. http://www.kittunstall.com

Also by Aurelia Skye

Alien Baby Pact

Baby For The Grimlock General

Baby For The Palantir Chief

Baby For The Brundle Commander

Baby For The Serp General

Alien Baby Pact Compilation

Baby For The Alphan Captain

Baby For The Mosaic Med Chief

Baby For The Tark Commander

Alien Baby Pakt

Alien Baby Pakt Zusammenstellung

BioCircuit Nexus

Cyborgs' Origins

Cyborg's Tether

Cyborg's Love

Celestial Mates
Wrong Place, Right Mate
Destined For The Drakari Warlords

Cybernetic Hearts
Mated To The Cyborg General
Claimed By The Cyborg Commander
Fated For The Cyborg Officer
Meant For The Cyborg Captain
Baby For The Cyborg General
Cybernetic Hearts: Complete Series
Cœurs Cybernétiques: Série Complète

Dazon Agenda
Written In The Stars
Alien's Babies
Diplomatic Affairs
Moon Madness
Across The Stars
Emperor's Assassin Bride
Dazon Agenda: Complete Collection
Compilation de l'Agenda Dazon

Evershift Haven

Pumpkin Spice and Orc's Delight
Howls & Harvest
Winter Wishes & Elven Kisses
A Snowstorm & A Stonehorn
Valentine's With A Vampire
Shamrocks & Second Chances
Eggsactly The Right Gargoyle
Barbells, Broomsticks & A Baby

Evershift Haven Serie, Edizione Italiana
Pumpkin Spice & Orc's Delight
Howls & Harvest – Edizione Italiana

Future Fairytales
Hooked

Guerriers Blessés
Chassé
Inlassable
Marqué
Justice
Compilation Guerriers Blessés

Harrow Bay

Hell Gates & Hot Flashes
Nightmares & Night Sweats
Warlocks & Wrinkles
Love Spells & Liver Spots
Phantasms & Presbyopia
Vampires & Varicose Veins
Mermaids & Mood Swings
Séances & Sagging Skin
Necromancy & Knee Pains
Marids & Memory Loss
Devil Deals & Dizzy Spells
Happy Endings & New Beginnings
Harrow Bay, Volume 1
Hellhounds & Mistletoe
Harrow Bay, Volume 2
Harrow Bay, Volume 3
Harrow Bay Complete Series

Harrow Bay, Édition Française
Hell Gates & Hot Flashes

Harrow Bucht Serie
Höllentore & Hitzewallungen
Alpträume Und Nachtschweiß
Hexenmeister & Falten
Liebeszauber Und Leberflecken
Phantasmen Und Alterssichtigkeit

Vampire und Krampfadern
Meerjungfrauen Und Stimmungsschwankungen
Séancen Und Schlaffe Haut
Nekromantie Und Knieschmerzen
Marids und Gedächtnisverlust
Teufelsgeschäfte Und Schwindelzauber
Happy Ends Und Neuanfängen
Höllenhunde & Mistelzweige

Hell Virus
Catching Hell
Surviving Hell
Bleeding Hell
Raising Hell
Sharing Hell

Howls Romance
The Jaguar Alpha's Forbidden Lover
CEO Wolf Shifter's Surprise Twins

Northstar Shifters
Northstar Heir's Scarred Mate

Olympus Station

Station Commander's Surrogate
Alien Prince's Secret Baby
Security Agent's Alien Bartender
Olympus Station Compilation

Pacte des Bébés Aliens
Compilation du Pacte des Bébés Aliens

SpicyShorts
Music In My Heart
Kilted Tentacle Monster: A Search for True Love

Sweet Escapes
Hook & Wendy

The Haunting of Clara Gray
Ghostly Awakening
Ghostly Harmonies

Three Crones Inn
Vastly Inn-proved
Ghastly Intentions

Grave Inn-tervention
Ghostly Inn-heritance
Three Crones Inn Compilation

Three Crones Inn (Drei Kronen Gasthaus)
GHOSTLY INN-TENTIONS (GEISTERHAFTES ERBE)

True North
True North #1: Death & Deception
True North #2: Rescued & Revelations
True North #3: Fire & Ice
True North #4: Enemies & Lovers
True North #5: Truth & Tiranog
True North #6: Fight & Flight
True North #7: Love & Loss

Wounded Warriors
Relentless
Marked
Justice
Wounded Warriors Collection
Hunted

Standalone

Reluctant Companion
Princess By Mistake
Fire Lord's Assistant
True North
Dragon Laird's Witch
Alien General's Rebel Consort
Tempted By Demons
Enemy Combatant
Grotesquerie
Mistaken Bounty
Wahre Richtung
Power Surges & Amorous Urges
Taken By The Orc General
Compilación Pacto de Alienígena Descendencia

Also by Juno Wells

Alien Baby Pact
Baby For The Grimlock General
Baby For The Palantir Chief
Baby For The Brundle Commander
Baby For The Serp General
Alien Baby Pact Compilation
Baby For The Alphan Captain
Baby For The Mosaic Med Chief
Baby For The Tark Commander

Alien Baby Pakt
Alien Baby Pakt Zusammenstellung

BioCircuit Nexus
Cyborgs' Origins
Cyborg's Tether
Cyborg's Love

Dazon Agenda
Written In The Stars
Alien's Babies
Diplomatic Affairs
Moon Madness
Across The Stars
Emperor's Assassin Bride
Dazon Agenda: Complete Collection
Compilation de l'Agenda Dazon

Galactic Alphas
Alpha's Omega
Buying His Omega
Claiming His Omega
Galactic Alphas Compilation

Pacte des Bébés Aliens
Compilation du Pacte des Bébés Aliens

Standalone
Alien General's Rebel Consort
Compilación Pacto de Alienígena Descendencia